Grumpy Bear

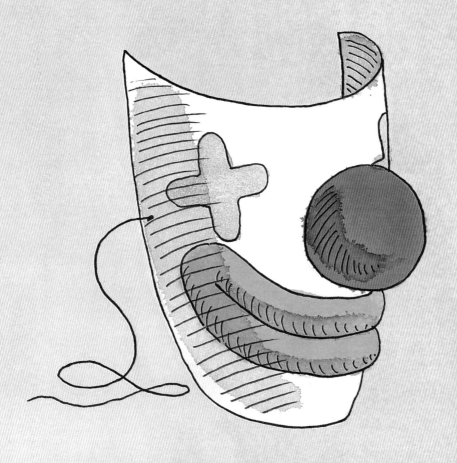

Written and Illustrated by Gavin Bishop

Big Bear worked as a clown,
but one day he was
feeling very grumpy.
"There are blisters on my feet,
and I've lost my curly wig,"
he grumbled.

3

Big Bear put on his coat.
He picked up his bag
and set off down the street.
"I hope I don't see anyone
I know," he said to himself.
"I'm too grumpy."

5

He hadn't gone far
when he saw Felix Fox.
"Oh dear," said Big Bear.
"I don't want Felix to see me
looking grumpy."

Big Bear opened his bag
and pulled out a clown mask.
He put it over his grumpy face.

"Good afternoon!" said Felix Fox.

Big Bear just nodded his head.

Felix Fox looked at Big Bear's
smiley face and felt happy.
"What a nice fellow,"
said Felix Fox to himself.

Next, Big Bear saw Rosie Rabbit and her little rabbits.

Big Bear opened his bag and pulled out some funny glasses and a big nose. He put them on his grumpy face.

"Good afternoon, Big Bear!"
said Rosie Rabbit.

Big Bear just nodded his head.

The little rabbits giggled at
Big Bear's funny face.

"Seeing Big Bear always makes
me feel happy," said Rosie Rabbit.

Big Bear was almost home
when he saw Colin Crocodile.

Big Bear opened his bag and took out another clown mask. He put it over his grumpy face.

"Hi there, old friend!"
said Colin Crocodile.

Big Bear just nodded his head.

"Big Bear always has a smile on his face," said Colin Crocodile to himself.

At last, Big Bear arrived at
his house. He still felt grumpy.
He went inside and hung up
his coat and his bag.

Then Big Bear looked in the mirror
and saw the funniest face
he had ever seen!

Big Bear laughed and laughed.

Little Bear came into the hall.
"What are you laughing at?"
she asked.

"I'm laughing at that funny bear!"
said Big Bear.

"But that's just you in the mirror!"
said Little Bear. "You still have
a mask on."

"I know," said Big Bear,
"but I didn't know
how funny I looked!"

23

Big Bear took off his mask.
He didn't feel grumpy at all!
"Let's have honey pancakes
for dinner," he said.